Come on

HUNTER DAVIES

Illustrated by
MALOU

Young Lions

Also in Young Lions

Flossie Teacake's Fur Coat
Flossie Teacake – Again!
Flossie Teacake Strikes Back!

First published in Great Britain in 1985
by The Bodley Head Ltd
First published in Young Lions 1987
8 Grafton Street, London W1X 3LA

Young Lions is an imprint of
the Collins Publishing Group

Text copyright © Hunter Davies 1985
Illustrations copyright © Malou 1985

Printed in Great Britain by
William Collins Sons & Co. Ltd, Glasgow

1

Introducing Ossie

Ossie was lying on his bedroom floor. He had been awake and out of bed for over an hour. Several times he had almost started to get himself dressed, but each time something incredible and amazing caught his attention. When this happened, he stopped, his mind completely absorbed, and he forgot what he was doing, which day it was, even which planet he was living on.

"Oswald," shouted a voice from downstairs. "Will you hurry yourself up!"

It was his mother. Ossie recognized that voice straight away. After all, she had been his mother for eleven years and five months and ten days so far. She was the best mother he'd come across during all that time. He should be able to recognize that voice by now.

Sometimes, Ossie wished she would take electrocution lessons, or whatever they were called, just to make her voice a bit softer and nicer. She was always shouting at him. She would do herself an injury one of these days. With a bit of luck. Nothing too serious, thought Ossie, just bad enough to have an Elastoplast over her gob for a few days so that none of those annoying words could come out, such as, "Oswald Do This, Oswald Do That."

"Oswald! I am not shouting for you any more!"

"Good," said Ossie, turning over another page. The incredible and amazing thing which had attracted his attention was a comic which he found he had not re-read that morning already.

Only Ossie's mother called Ossie Oswald. That was what he had been christened, Oswald Osgood. It was the most stupid name Ossie had ever heard. Really soppy and babyish. Imagine *anyone* calling *anyone* Oswald. If he had been at the christening, he would have told his mother how really stupid she was.

Well, he had been at the christening, but he had had other things to do that day. Such as screaming his little head off. His mother had told him this story hundreds of times — and that he had gone on to scream his head off for the first five years of his life. Ossie was fed up with hearing these stupid stories. Ossie's favourite word was "stupid". Everyone and everything he didn't like was stupid.

Ossie would really like to have been called Kevin or Wayne, or Darren or Glenn—really good names, the sort of names real people had, not that stupid Oswald name. There were two Darrens in his class at school, plus a Glenn and a Wayne. In his whole year, which consisted of six classes of eleven-year-old boys and girls, he estimated there were dozens and dozens of Darrens and Waynes. In fact he knew millions of boys with really good names. Yet *he* had to get lumbered with Oswald.

According to his mother, there had once been a Saint called Oswald and it was a very Old English name. Ossie would have much preferred a New English name. But the real reason for the choice had been to please his grandfather, whose name it was.

At primary school, his nickname had been Snotty, and if you really wanted to upset him you called him Snotty Bum Bum—but that had been ages ago. Now he was generally known as Ossie.

At one time, he denied all knowledge of being called Oswald, in any form, but when his favourite football team, Tottenham Hotspur, signed an Argentinian player who turned out to be called Ossie, overnight he revealed to the world what his true name was. Well, not quite. He still hated Oswald. But Ossie was bearable.

Eventually, when he was grown up, say around eighteen, he would call himself Oz. Much more muscular. There was something a bit weedy about Ossie.

With a great struggle, standing on one leg holding his comic in one hand, Ossie managed at last to pull on one sock.

This was a most difficult manoeuvre. Putting on any clothes, when you can only use one hand and you are looking in another direction and your mind is miles away, is exceedingly complicated. Ossie hoped that one of these days there would be a TV competition for getting dressed with your eyes shut. He would be sure to win.

Then he sank to the floor again and continued reading. He was now dressed in his underpants and one sock. Not bad going, for just over an hour of getting up and getting ready to face the world.

"Oswald! If you are not down in five minutes . . ."

That woman again. Where did she get her energy from? She should rest her voice, thought Ossie. She might need it one day for something *really* urgent. If we were invaded by space men and little green monsters came down the chimney and ran all over her new carpet, she might have something to shout about. Till then, she should save it. That would be his advice. But nobody ever asked Ossie's advice about anything. All of them being completely stupid, they never would.

"Oswald, I am coming up to get you, and if you are not dressed . . ."

"Oh God, woman," shouted Ossie. "Course I'm dressed. What do you think I've been doing all morning? I've been dressed for hours."

With that, Ossie put down his comic, a two-month-old copy of the *Beano,* and quickly pulled on his other sock. But not quite. The toe was left hanging off by about four inches. Ossie had noticed in the pile of comics beside him last week's *Eagle*.

He had not re-read that for—well, it must be at least half an hour. Better give it another quick bash.

"Ouch, gerroff. Stop it, woman. That hurts!" Mrs Osgood had come into Ossie's bedroom, taken one look at him lying half naked on his bedroom floor completely surrounded by a sea of comics, and was dragging him up by his bare arm.

Ossie had very thin arms. He also had very thin legs. In fact he was very thin and weedy all over. This was a great worry to Ossie, and a great puzzle to his mother. He ate like a horse, even if not always the right sort of food, but he never seemed to grow any bigger or any fatter.

His grandfather told Ossie not to worry. He hadn't grown till he was sixteen. It was perfectly normal. Not to worry. He had worn short trousers till he was fifteen, so he said, which was very useful for getting into everything at half price. Ossie was not at all impressed. He wanted to be big *now*. He wouldn't mind paying full price, if it meant getting into pubs and adult films and riding motorbikes.

"I knew you weren't dressed yet," said Mrs Osgood.

"How can I get dressed, with you torturing me? Look at the bruises. My arm is all blue. I'm reporting you. Murderer. Vivisectionist. Arsonist . . . "

Ossie sat on his bed, calling her nearly all the worst names he could think of. He did know far worse things to call people, and sometimes shouted them in the playground, as the other boys did, though most of them he did not quite understand. But if he used them at home to his mother, he knew there would be big trouble.

"Hurry up!" she said. "I am not leaving this room till you are completely dressed."

"I think you've broke it. Look, I can't move this arm. All your stupid fault. I am reporting you, the RSPCA prosecute people like you."

"That's for animals," said his mother.

"That's what *you* are. A ferocious animal, attacking me like that."

"No, the RSPCA protects animals. You're getting mixed up."

"*You* are the one mixed up, if you ask me. A mixed-up old woman. You rush in here, attack me like an animal, stop me just when I'm getting dressed . . ."

"Look, I haven't come up here to argue."

"You started the stupid argument. Typical, just typical . . ."

Very slowly, Ossie got dressed, taking care to move his right arm very gently, the one he claimed had been broken.

"What's all the hurry anyway?" said Ossie. "You know it's Saturday. Remember? No school today. You always get into such a panic. There's no hurry at all, yet you rush into *my* bedroom, attacking me like a loony."

"Yes, I know it's Saturday, smarty boots. Which is why your grandad will be waiting for you."

"Oh," started Ossie. He had indeed completely forgotten about his grandad. It was his weekly job, to help his grandad on Saturday morning, but every Saturday morning he forgot all about it.

"Oh, yes, I know," said Ossie. "But he told me last week there was no hurry. Just come round when I'm ready. That's what he told me. Honest. He hates people like you, who rush rush rush all the time. He told me. And I agree with him. The trouble with you, Mum, is that you are just a P-A-I-N . . ."

"Very good. Now what about the rest of your spelling homework," said Mrs Osgood. "Have you done that yet?"

"It's for Monday morning, stupid," said Ossie. "This is only Saturday, woman. Give me a break. Please."

Ossie's younger sister Lucy was in the kitchen, sitting at the kitchen table, doing a lovely drawing for her grandfather. She of course had been up for hours, and had already dressed and re-dressed several times. Later that morning she was going to her acting class, and she always went through several changes of clothing before deciding on the right outfit to stun her friends with.

"Morning, Luce," said Ossie. He was always very kind and pleasant to his little sister, always protective and considerate. Well, most of the time.

"Shush," said Lucy, throwing back her long golden hair with a twist of her neck, a trick she had worked on for weeks to perfect. "Can't you see I'm working, Ossie?"

"Oh God, can't even talk in this house," said Ossie. "*I* don't complain if people talk or shout or scream or anything. Personally, I like lots and lots of noise when I'm working."

"*When* you're working," said Mrs Osgood. "People have to be very quick to catch *you* working."

"Look, are you going to moan at me all day? Supposed to have a day of rest. Supposed to have a break after a hard week at that stupid school, but you go on and on all the time."

"Sorry I spoke, your majesty."

Ossie climbed up to the breakfast bar to have his breakfast. It was in a corner of the kitchen, all done in white plastic, which Ossie was very fond of. He started to whistle, pretending he was at a real bar, sipping pints of real beer.

"Mum, tell him to stop," said Lucy.

"What have I done now? Should I stop breathing? Is that what you want? You just want me to stop breathing. OK, I will. Then you'll be sorry. You'll rush to give me the kiss of life, but it will be too late. I'll have been asphyxiointed."

"I don't think anyone will rush to give you kisses, Ossie," said Lucy, very carefully writing Grandad's name at the top of the card with her best felt pen.

Happy Birthday Dear Grandad.

"Creep," said Ossie. "Double creep. It's not his birthday for yonks."

That was one of Ossie's latest words, yonks. He had used it continuously for a whole week. This was the normal length of time Ossie manhandled any word or phrase. After about a week, he dropped them, by which time they were so battered and bruised they were not much use to anyone else. Ossie had knocked all sense out of them.

"I'll have two fried eggs, and three rashers of bacon," shouted Ossie. "Some fried bread and tomatoes. Come on. Chop, chop, woman."

Mrs Osgood was in the kitchen part of the kitchen. Lucy was still very busy with her drawing, putting a border round it with a glitter pen.

"Mum, are you listening? I've been sitting here for yonks. Oh yes, you were the one said hurry up. You were the one said I'd be late. Now it's you keeping me back."

Mrs Osgood came across to the breakfast bar and handed Ossie a small bowl of muesli and one small slice of wholemeal toast. During the week, Ossie and Lucy had to get their own breakfasts because Mrs Osgood went out to work, but on Saturdays, if she was in a good mood, she usually served them.

"I can't eat this muck," said Ossie, starting on it at once.

"What are you going to do with it, then?" said

Lucy, looking up. "Stick it up your bum bum, Snotty Bum Bum."

"Mum, did you *hear* that?" shouted Ossie. "Did you hear what Lucy said? Oh yes, you tell me off, but you never tell her off."

"Two minutes, Oswald," shouted his mother from the living room.

There was then silence. Lucy had returned to her drawing and Ossie, having polished off his meagre breakfast in two seconds, had pulled up his jumper to reveal two old *Beanos*. He had shoved them there, emergency supplies, for when he might need them. He spread both of them out on the white plastic surface of the bar, pushing the dirty bowl and plate aside, and started to read.

He didn't hear his mother come back into the kitchen, but suddenly he felt his arm violently grabbed, the sore arm which had already been maltreated that morning.

"Oswald Osgood, you are a selfish pig," shouted his mother, pulling him down from the breakfast bar and sweeping both his comics on to the floor. Then she gave an even louder yell.

"And look at that! Those filthy comics have left

ink all over the place. Look at the marks. I've just wiped it. They'll never come off. I have warned you enough times not to read at meals."

"Not my fault," said Ossie. "I don't print them. Don't blame me. Blame the stupid printers."

"Get out of the kitchen," said his mother.

"It was your fault anyway," said Ossie. "You must of left the surface wet, that's what. That's why it's picked up the ink. See, it's still all wet. Your fault. You must of left it wet . . ."

"Must 'have'," corrected his mother. "How many times have I got to tell you."

"I dunno. You can count. You went to school."

"One of these days, my lad, you will go too far. Your poor grandfather has been waiting for you for hours. You have no thought for anyone but yourself."

She frog-marched Ossie to the back door, opened it with one hand, then pushed him out, closing the door firmly behind him.

"When I'm grown up," thought Ossie, "and I'm in charge of everything, I'll have comics delivered every day. And I'll read them with my bacon and eggs. Every morning . . ."

*

Ossie was riding his BMX Raleigh Burner GX. It had been his Christmas present last year, which of course was yonks ago, and Ossie considered it was now really too small for him.

"It's not fair, having to put up with this old thing. If only I was older and had a proper bike, like a Suzuki. This hasn't even got any decent accessories. I know some kids with so many extras you can hardly see their bikes at all."

He was riding on the pavement, something he was not supposed to do. All the neighbours had complained about BMXs being ridden up and down the pavements, upsetting old people and frightening the little kids.

Ossie was riding no hands and whistling, showing off. Then he tried a few wheelies, though not very good ones.

"How can I do proper wheelies on this wreck? If I had a proper machine, I'd be the best biker in the whole world. Then they'd all see."

He turned the corner rather too quickly and fell slap into the arms of Flossie Teacake.

She was a large girl, though she was the same age as Ossie and was in his class. He didn't really care for her. She had moved recently from London and she was always boasting about it. Ossie often walked to school with her, if by chance they met on the way, but he made sure he wasn't seen actually going through the gates with her.

"You stupid fool," said Ossie, picking himself off the ground. "Couldn't you see me coming?"

"Couldn't you look where you're going?" said Flossie.

"That's the second arm I've had broken this morning."

"Shall I get my bike out and play?" asked Flossie.

"No," said Ossie. "I am going to work."

"You don't go to work," said Flossie. "You haven't got a job. What a liar, Ossie Osgood."

Ossie's grandfather's home was only two streets away, on the same new estate. He lived in what was called Sheltered Housing.

When Ossie had first heard about this, he thought it would be some sort of encampment, with a big open fire, horses tied up against trees, and his grandad living in his own wigwam, the biggest and best wigwam of course, with full colour telly, only

22

the best being good enough for Ossie's grandfather.

Ossie had been somewhat disappointed to find that it was a rather boring concrete block, full of old people. Ossie's grandfather had one living room, with a bathroom and a little bedroom. But inside his tiny flat Ossie's grandfather looked after himself, doing his own cooking and cleaning. There was a bell he could ring, if he ever wanted help, but he never did. Ossie's grandfather was very independent.

He had trouble walking: that was his only real problem so far as Ossie could see—something to do with arthritis in his ankles. Some days he could walk all the way to the pub and back. Sometimes he couldn't. It wasn't very far. The pub was next door.

His memory was also not so good as it used to be, though that, too, came and went. His old memory was excellent. It was his new memory which was not so good. Things which had happened to him yesterday often went straight out of his mind, but things which had happened forty or fifty or even sixty years ago were absolutely clear. Ossie liked to hear these memories, especially the stories about wartime. Those were the best.

As Ossie came to the pub beside his grandad's home, he heard someone shouting at him.

"Snoopy One Two. Are you receiving me? Snoopy One Two. Are you receiving me?"

It sounded a bit like Snotty Bum Bum. Could someone know his old nickname? Ossie stopped and looked around. Who on earth could be calling him?

He got off his BMX and looked up and down the street. The pub was full. It was Saturday and the pub had just opened for the lunch-time trade, but there was no one around outside.

Ossie suddenly realized there was a huge motorbike parked nearby. It was a Suzuki GS 1000. Ossie had a photograph of it at home above his bed, torn out of a comic, so he knew it well. It was red, white and blue, the colours he planned to have if he ever got a bike, if he ever lived to be eighteen.

"Snoopy One Two. Are you receiving me?"

Ossie realized the words were coming from the motorbike. He knew that the Japanese made amazing motorbikes, but he didn't know that these days they could make them talk. "Brilliant, these Japanese."

Ossie went nearer, felt the throttle, admired the

wheels, moved his hand down the body. He almost jumped in the air when the voice spoke again.

"Look, stop messing around, Snoopy One Two. What the hell are you playing at? Roger and out."

Ossie now saw that it was the motorbike's radio which was blaring away. Ossie looked around, but could see no signs of a rider, or of anyone else. Very slowly, he picked up the mouthpiece from its little cradle on the front of the bike.

As he did so, a very large and spotty youth dressed all in leather, wearing enormous heavy boots, stuck his head out of the pub door.

"You touch that bike, you little swine," he shouted, "and I'll have you."

Ossie jumped on his own bike, his BMX, so small that it looked like a toy bike by comparison, and rode as fast as he could straight into his grandfather's block.

Ossie let himself into his grandfather's flat. For his eleventh birthday, he had been given a key ring with three keys on it—for his own front door, his grandad's flat and his locker at school. He kept the keys on a string round his neck. If he lost them, his mother had warned, it would be a hanging offence.

"Sorry I'm late, Grandad," said Ossie. "It was Mum's fault. She made me do so many jobs."

"I'd given you up for lost," said his grandad. He was sitting in front of the gas fire, which he kept on all the year round, watching television. It was horse-racing. Grandad was watching with the sound off, as he always did. He hated all commentators and experts of any sort.

"What do you want, anyway?" he grunted. "I've got nothing for you, so don't ask."

"I've come to help you," said Ossie.

"Help, it's not help I want. A new pair of legs, that's all I need, then I'll be off out of this dump."

Ossie stood waiting, looking round the room. Every Saturday morning he was late, sometimes very late, and every Saturday morning he had to put up with his grandad's moans.

Ossie knew it was the old man's way of paying him back for being late. Grandad hated unpunctuality, among many other things.

"Do you want me to go to the shops, Grandad?"

"Why?" asked Grandad, changing channels to wrestling, then back again to the horse-racing.

"So you can have food. So you can eat."

"Oh, bit late to think of that. No point in me eating. I'll be dying soon. What's the point of eating? Waste of good food. I hate to see good food being wasted. Would you like a bacon sandwich?"

Ossie had not been listening properly, but at the

mention of a bacon sandwich he was all attention.

"Yes, please, Grandad. If you have any."

"I *did* have plenty," said his grandad, getting up from his chair and going to his little stove. "But I thought *you* were never coming. I ate most of it myself. Oh, you're in luck. Enough for one sandwich only. Sauce?"

That was another thing Ossie was not allowed at home. HP sauce. In fact he was not allowed sauce of any kind.

Grandad watched with pleasure as Ossie wolfed it all down.

"That's the stuff. No wonder you're a little skinny-ma-link, with all that rabbit food she gives you. Lots of eggs and bacon, that's the stuff to put hairs on your chest."

"I haven't even got a chest," said Ossie. "That's what . . ."

Before he could finish his sentence, Grandad had burst into such laughter, spluttering and slapping himself, coughing and choking, that Ossie thought he was going to have a heart attack.

"Not even got . . ." spluttered Grandad, "a . . . chest . . ."

There were tears rolling down his cheeks. He took out his false teeth (a sight which Ossie hated) to help himself breathe, then he put them back in again.

"Right, that's enough from you, boyo," said Grandad, suddenly becoming serious. "Here, cop hold of this."

From his pocket, he produced a neatly written list of shopping, a five-pound note and a plastic carrier bag.

"Now off you go. Can't you see I'm trying to watch the racing?"

When Ossie went shopping with his mother, the big shopping which she did every two weeks, they went to Tesco and needed a whole trolley to carry all their stuff. For his grandad's weekend shopping, all Ossie needed was a small wire basket. Even then, the food hardly covered the bottom of the basket.

The supermarket was very near, right next to the pub, and as usual there was a huge queue for the one till at the end of the shop. It was all so stupid, so Ossie thought, going *out* shopping. When he was older and could afford a proper computer, he would do his own program and order all the shopping, just by sitting at home.

Ossie quickly picked up his grandad's packet of streaky bacon, half a dozen eggs, half a pound of butter, half a pound of Cheddar cheese and a white loaf, thick-sliced. The order was the same every week.

Every day of his life, Grandad cooked himself bacon and eggs for breakfast. He often ate the same for lunch as well, if the Meals-on-Wheels people brought something he thought was revolting, which he did most of the time. Sometimes he had bacon and eggs again for his tea. Then, just before bed, he had toasted cheese.

Toasted cheese before bed, Ossie's mother always told him, gave you bad dreams. And as for bacon and eggs, every newspaper and magazine agreed that they were very bad for you indeed.

Sometimes, Ossie thought, it would be really good to be old right now.

"When you're old, you can eat anything you like and no one tells you off."

It seemed to take ages to get to the till. People pushed ahead of him in the queue, then kept leaving it for things they had forgotten, each time coming back into the queue ahead of Ossie, not going to the end, where he thought they should be.

"That's the worst of being small. People think you don't exist."

When he did get to the top of the queue, a big fat blonde woman behind him got served first. The grumpy shopkeeper behind the till, who was an enemy of Ossie's anyway, smiled and said he hadn't seen Ossie hiding below the counter.

"Why don't you grow up a bit quicker?" he said, with a leer on his face.

"Why don't you drop dead?" replied Ossie, grabbing his change and running out of the shop.

"Here you are, Grandad. Got your stuff."

His grandad was still watching the television. It was now the football previews, so Ossie sat down with him.

"What a load of rubbish," said Ossie. "Gerroff. You don't want to watch that rubbish."

On the screen some Arsenal players were being interviewed. Ossie pretended to put his hands over his eyes.

"I can't watch. Tell me when they've been put down, Grandad."

Then there was a preview of that afternoon's Spurs' match, so Ossie naturally jumped up and cheered everything any Spurs said or did.

As he and his grandad watched the programme together, they each kept up a running commentary, but neither was really talking to the other.

Grandad suspected and disliked all modern footballers, regardless of their team or country. All the way through he shouted out "Big head". Then he would click his tongue and shake his head.

"Publicity. That's all he's doing it for. And the money. Big heads. The lot of them."

Ossie was equally clear-cut in his views. He approved of everything his favourite players said or did, which meant everyone who played for Spurs and everyone who played for England, unless they happened to come from Arsenal. In that case, all he did was boo and jeer.

After it was over, Grandad pulled out a bag of sweets from the side of his chair and gave one to Ossie.

When he wasn't eating fried bacon and eggs,

Grandad was stuffing himself with boiled sweets, really hard ones, the sort that almost break your teeth. Ossie's mother did not allow these in her house either. Lethal, she called them.

"My mum," said Ossie, "she says that all the good things in life are bad for you."

Grandad appeared to choke on a sweet, but just managed to recover.

"I'll put your stuff away, Grandad," said Ossie, getting up.

"Don't bother," said Grandad. "I'll manage."

"No, no, Mum said I should do more to help."

Ossie went to his grandad's little fridge, which was on a shelf beside his draining board, and put away the shopping.

Grandad was most surprised. Usually Ossie just dumped things down anywhere and left them.

The reason Ossie was so helpful today was that he feared he had broken the eggs, running out of the shop in such a hurry. He wanted them put away in the fridge before his grandad found out.

"Anything else then? I'll have to be off. Mum

wants me to do some more jobs. It's all I ever do. Work, work, work."

"Here," said his grandad rather gruffly. "I've got something to show you. Close your eyes."

Ossie was suspicious. His grandad often did play nasty tricks on him, shoving horrible-tasting things in his mouth when Ossie thought he was getting a sweet. He had once bitten through a whole piece of coal, thinking it was barley sugar. Grandad had nearly died of laughing.

"Come with me," said his grandad. "No looking, now."

Ossie closed his eyes and felt his hand being taken. He was led into the hall where Grandad fumbled with the door of his bedroom.

Grandad allowed nobody near his bedroom, in case the Germans found out about it. That was what he told Ossie. Ossie rather liked Germans. After England, they were his best football team, though France was also pretty good these days. He would quite like to see the German football team arriving and going into Grandad's bedroom. That would be something to tell all those stupid kids in his class at school.

"Shush now," said Grandad. "Not a word to anyone."

The sight which met Ossie's eyes was unbelievable. It looked to him like a museum: but a mad museum, because things were piled so high on every surface that at first there seemed no space even to stand and look.

He took a while to work out where the bed was. It was pushed into a corner and was almost completely covered in bundles of old newspapers, tied up with string. There were cases and boxes everywhere, all crammed with things, and clothes and objects hung from every wall.

Grandad had only agreed to come to this Sheltered Housing on condition that he could bring his own things. As he had never thrown out a newspaper for thirty years, this had proved very difficult. He and Ossie's mother had had endless rows about it, but in the end Grandad had managed to bring with him the best part of his treasures.

"Now don't touch," said Grandad. "I know where everything is."

"Is it all yours, Grandad? It's amazing."

"It is," said Grandad. "And when you're eighteen, I might let you have a few things. But I'm not promising."

On some dusty shelves, Ossie could see bundles of old envelopes marked "Active Service—Army Privileged Envelope". Some of them were stamped "Passed by Censor". There were also some ration books and faded photographs of groups of soldiers.

At the back of a shelf, Ossie was sure he could see a dagger. There was even what seemed to be the handle of a pistol, sticking out from a holster. They all looked German, perhaps kept from the War. That might be why he didn't want the Germans to know.

"Don't you ever tell anyone about this lot, my lad," said Grandad.

"No, I won't, Grandad," said Ossie. "Honest."

"Right, if you want to have a look around, I'll give you ten minutes. I'm going to have some tea. But don't take anything. It's all been counted."

Ossie stood for a long time on his own. The bedroom was very dark and it had taken him some time to get properly adjusted to the gloom. The reason

36

for the darkness, he now discovered, was that the biggest wardrobe he had ever seen had been shoved up against the window.

"A whole platoon could get inside that," thought Ossie. "Perhaps a whole regiment."

It was made of very dark mahogany wood, gleaming and shiny, so that he could see his own reflection in it. It was obviously the only piece of furniture in the bedroom which his grandfather kept clean and dusted.

Very carefully, Ossie worked his way across the room, climbing over the bed, pushing aside some of the cases, crawling round the boxes. When he got beside it, he felt dwarfed. It was like an enormous brown giant towering over him.

"Shall I open it?" thought Ossie. "All he said was not to take anything. I won't break anything, just look."

Ossie slowly opened the wardrobe, then gently he stepped inside. The door swung behind him with a creak. He took fright at first, but he waited, listened, and then grew braver.

Through some cracks in the thinner sheets of wood at the back of the wardrobe shone strange

shafts of light, just enough to make the inside not totally black.

Ossie felt around him. With his hands, he could make out what might be uniforms, with badges and decorations on them. Stretching further, he felt something very solid and cold, smooth enough to be flesh. He gave a little scream.

"Perhaps it's a body! A dead body. Inside one of the uniforms . . ."

He pressed harder with both hands, then realized he was touching a pair of well-polished leather boots, the sort cavalry officers used to wear.

"Wish I was old enough to be a soldier," thought Ossie. "I could put on those boots, right now."

He began to feel slightly dizzy, overcome by the eerie darkness and by the mysterious atmosphere. There was a moisty smell of mothballs mixed with old clothes, of leather and polish, and perhaps even (or was he imagining it?) of guns and gunpowder.

"Oh, if only I was eighteen this minute," said Ossie. "Why have I got to wait till I'm grown up. I want to be GROWN now. And UP there. Big and strong. Not small and weedy. Oh, it's not fair."

His left hand suddenly touched something

smooth and hard, some sort of metal. He felt the shape of it. It seemed like a cross; perhaps it was an Iron Cross? Then he felt something jagged and sharp. A bit of shrapnel perhaps? And that round thing, it couldn't be a hand-grenade, could it?

"I'd better get out quick. The police will be after all this lot, not just the Germans."

But Ossie didn't move. After all these years, he decided that nothing would start exploding now, or so he hoped.

He found himself unable to move anyway. It was as if he had been hypnotized, standing there in the dark for so long, breathing in all the strange smells, excited by the darkness and dankness of the wardrobe, half scared by all the dangerous objects, and all the time wishing he was eighteen and grown-up, able to try on all the uniforms.

As he stood there he closed his eyes, holding the Iron Cross with both hands. He then began to feel his body trembling. He thought at first it was fright, but he no longer felt afraid. It felt more as if his body was moving, as if it was expanding, changing of its own accord.

He opened the door of the wardrobe a few inches,

enough to let some light in, and quickly looked at himself in the mirror inside the door. He was shocked by what he saw. A miraculous transformation had taken place. Looking back at him from the mirror was a boy six foot tall, very strong-looking and very well built.

Inside his body, and inside his mind, he still felt like an eleven-year-old. He knew where he was, and who he was. But, on the outside, he had suddenly moved forward in time and had taken on the form and the figure of himself, seven years ahead. Or was he imagining it?

"Grandad," he shouted. "I think I'll go now."

His voice was very deep. He looked around for a moment, wondering where it had come from, but he was the only person in the room.

There was no reply from his grandad. He must be watching television again.

"I'm off," he said, but not too loudly.

He let himself out of the bedroom, went into the hall, then ran out of the block, just as fast as his eighteen-year-old legs could carry him.

2

Ossie and the Super Bike

It was still there. Oz stood on the pavement admiring it. It was still as gleaming and powerful as it had seemed when he first looked at it. Now that he was eighteen, he was at least looking *down* on it, rather than gazing up at it.

"Very handy, being six foot. It gives you a whole different view on life," thought Oz.

Now, of course, that he was grown-up, he would be called Oz. By everyone. He would soon thump anyone who dared to use any silly, childish names or nicknames, when he was around.

"Snoopy One Two, Snoopy One Two. This is an Emergency. Urgent. This is an Emergency. Snoopy One Two."

Oz looked towards the pub door. He could just faintly see the outline of the motorbike rider, who was now slumped against the bar. He was obviously not able to ride his bike, not if he had been drinking beer all this time, or shorts, or Black and Tans, or Black Ladies. Oz was not quite sure what you did drink, once you got to eighteen, but perhaps he would soon find out.

"Snoopy One Two. This is an Emergency."

Oz picked up the radio receiver and put it to his mouth.

"One, two, three, testing," said Oz. "Hello, hello. One, two, three, testing . . ."

Oz had once heard his scout-master at a scout concert testing the microphone. Or was it "Mary Had a Little Lamb" that you recited? He wasn't sure.

"One, two, three, testing . . ." began Oz again, but a tremendous buzzing noise made him jump.

"Who the hell's that?" said a very angry voice.

"It's Snoopy One Two," said Oz. "Sorry about that. I am receiving you. Roger and In . . ."

"About time," said the very angry voice. "Where have you been?"

"Sorry, I had to help me grandad, I mean this old feller. He had a heart attack. I gave him the kiss of life, he's all right now, the police have got him, I'll probably get a medal."

"What the hell are you talking about?"

"I am receiving you," said Oz. "Ready for Action. Over and out."

Oz stood for a while, looking at the giant motorbike, trying to remember all the instruments and controls. Very slowly he put on the enormous crash helmet which the rider had left slung over the radio aerial at the back of the bike. Then he took it off again.

The angry voice was still giving messages, but Oz couldn't hear a thing with the helmet on. Especially as he had put it on back to front, which meant he couldn't see either.

He replaced it the right way round; now he could hear much better. Then he picked up the microphone again.

"Please repeat message," said Oz. "I missed that. Sorry. Police came back to give me my medal. Ready and Out, Roger . . ."

"Look stop messing about, Snoopy One Two. You have to go at once to 149 Park Road and pick up an urgent package. Is that clear?"

"Message received," said Oz, putting the receiver back on its holder. He quickly tied up his helmet and looked for the key. Luckily, it had been left in the ignition.

Oz wished he had spent longer studying the photograph in his bedroom. He knew the right hand was the throttle and the left was the clutch. At his right foot was the brake and at his left foot the gears. But could he work them all together?

He stood for some time revving up the engine, to get the feel of the controls. The engine grew noisier and noisier, though Oz could not hear the worst of it through his helmet. He had never realized helmets were so large and effective. He felt like a space man. And with the enormous, powerful, urgent monster between his legs, he felt as if he was sitting on a space rocket.

At last, with an enormous roar, Oz managed to slip into gear, turn up the throttle, and then whoosh, he was off.

Broom, broom, broom!

Oz had set off so quickly that he did not have time to think about steering.

The monster motorbike roared straight ahead and before Oz could stop it, it had mounted the pavement and was through the front door of the supermarket, the one where Oz had gone to do his grandfather's shopping.

"Clear the way!" shouted Oz, going down the main aisle. "Urgent business! Clear the way."

The queue, as ever, was very long, but all the customers made a dash for the wall, throwing themselves against it for protection.

The grumpy man on the till looked terrified and crouched on the floor. As Oz roared past him, he put out his hand and pressed all the buttons on his till at once, ringing up several hundred pounds.

Oz used his foot to slow himself down, looking for the other door of the shop, which he knew was somewhere at the back, and as he did so his foot caught the bottom row of some large-size packets of Automatic Persil. The whole pile immediately started crashing down.

The grumpy shopkeeper lifted his head above the till, groaned, then disappeared again.

"Serves him right," thought Oz to himself. "If he was kinder to eleven-year-olds, eighteen-year-olds might be kinder to him."

Oz managed to turn the front wheel and just missed plunging straight into the largest deep freeze, which could have been uncomfortable. Even with his crash helmet on.

"What are you looking for?" said a little girl of about ten, one of Lucy's friends, as Oz came to a stop.

"Streaky bacon," said Oz. "I always go like a blue streak, when I'm looking for streaky bacon."

"Is this some sort of promotional stunt?" said an old man, coming up.

"This week's Special Offer," said Oz. "Buy me and ride one."

Oz got the Suzuki started again, roared round the counters, slowed down at the cakes to put a rum baba in his mouth, then he found the side door and zoomed into the shop's back yard, scattering piles of empty boxes and crates. He speeded round the yard a few times, then crashed through an old wooden back door into the main road again.

Oz roared along a dual carriage-way at about fifty miles an hour. He was at last getting the hang of the controls. At roundabouts, he was enjoying creeping up beside cars on the inside, then sneakily getting ahead, leaving them behind.

"Here comes Oz! Watch out everybody!"

At traffic lights he hardly ever had to stop, roaring down the outside of the long lines of waiting cars, getting away first just as the lights changed, sometimes without even having to change gear.

"Here comes Oz! The Wizard on the Bike!"

There was an equally fast-looking motorbike ahead of him, painted white, by the look of it, though Oz's helmet was now slipping a bit and his vision was not as good as it should have been. Oz accelerated to catch up.

"Here he comes! The Wizard of Oz!"

Oz had done quite a few miles by now, some of them very quickly, and he felt confident enough to give this other bike a bit of a race.

"Zoom, zoom!" said Oz, as he opened the throttle. "Broom, broom!"

As he came alongside the other motorbike, he noticed that it too had a long aerial. It must be a motorbike messenger as well, thought Oz.

Oz gave the rider a wave.

"I'm Snoopy One Two," he shouted. "But you can call me Oz."

Oz looked back at the side of the bike to see what firm it belonged to. The name seemed to begin with the letter P. He had whizzed past so quickly that he hadn't looked properly, so he slowed down to let it catch up with him.

He then noticed that on the side of the white motorbike was written the word *Police*.

"Snoopy One Two. Where the hell are you?"

Oz had forgotten he was supposed to be on an urgent call. He stopped and picked up the receiver.

"Don't mess around with me, my lad," said the policeman. He had got off his white motorbike and was standing beside Oz, getting out his notebook.

"Sorry, Officer," said Oz, "Your Worship. But it's an emergency, honest. Had to go as fast as possible. The boss told me . . ."

"How old are you?" said the policeman. "And where's your licence?"

"Snoopy One Two," crackled the voice on the receiver. "Downing Street is waiting for you. They're going mad. Over and out."

The policeman stopped, looking rather puzzled.

So was Oz, but he tried not to show it.

"Snoopy One Two reporting," said Oz, picking up the microphone, looking as important and as professional as he could.

"That wretched parcel is for the Prime Minister," shouted the voice. "She left it yesterday at Brookfield School. You've got to get it on the 12.45 London train, so get a bloody move on, Snoopy One Two. Roger and out."

Oz smiled, putting the receiver back on its holder. The policeman's expression had changed completely.

"Sorry about the bad language, Officer," said Oz. "They do get a bit over-excited at times, at headquarters. But as you heard, it is for the PM. So if you don't mind, I'd better . . ."

"That's right," said the officer. "She was at Brookfield School yesterday. She must have left something. Oh well then, you'd better get along, son. But don't go *too* fast."

"Thank you, Officer," said Oz, jumping on his bike again, roaring away, but sticking to the speed limit this time. Just in case.

*

"I should have realized," thought Oz as he roared along the main road. "Number One Four Nine Park Road. That's next door to Brookfield. My old school. It must be the number of Miss Henn's house."

Now that he knew exactly where he was going, Oz took a few short cuts and rode into the playground by a back entrance. It was playtime and he was immediately surrounded by a crowd of kids. He recognized most of them.

"Give us a ride," said one of them.

"Can you do any tricks?" said another.

"Come on, mister, let's talk into your machine."

Oz was busy showing off, explaining a few of the instruments, when across the playground he could see Miss Henn, dashing out of her private gate and rushing towards him.

"Where on earth have you been?" she screamed at him. "I've been waiting ages. This is rather vital, you know."

Oz got off his bike and stood up properly. Miss Henn had always been a very bossy headmistress and he had been rather scared of her not so very long ago. He was worried now she might tell him off for

something, just as in the old days.

"Sorry, Miss," said Oz. "I know I should have brought a note from my mum to say why I was late . . ."

"What on earth are you talking about?"

She looked into Oz's face. He was sure she was

going to recognize him, but with his helmet on he did look rather different. And of course he was now six feet tall.

"Look here, the Prime Minister forgot this yesterday when she was opening the new wing. I think it's her handbag. Take great care of it."

"Is that all?" said Oz. "All that fuss for a titchy parcel."

"It is frightfully important," said Miss Henn. "It has to be on the twelve forty-five London train. You do know where the station is, don't you?"

"Course I do," said Oz. "Been there lots of times train-spotting."

"At your age!" said Miss Henn.

"No, I mean when I was eleven. Yonks ago."

Oz took the parcel and roared off in the direction of the station. It was by now 12.35. He had only ten minutes to get there, so he opened the throttle as far as it would go and was very soon touching seventy miles an hour as he roared down the main road.

He had to slow down a bit when he got near the station, to about fifty, but he was still going very fast and people turned to stare at him, shaking their heads and waving their fists at him. Oz waved back.

He thought they were congratulating him on his riding.

"Hold on, train," he shouted. "Here comes Oz! Broom, broom, broom."

Oz rode straight into the station entrance and right through the barrier. The London train was already on the far platform.

"Here, where's your ticket?" shouted the ticket collector, so surprised he had let Oz go straight through.

"You can't ride a bike in here," shouted a porter.

"Life and death, mate," said Oz, dodging through the trolleys and zooming over a bridge. "Parcel for the PM. They're waiting for it at Euston. Secret Service. MI5. KGB. BBC. RSPCA."

The whistle went, the doors were being closed, and it was obvious that the train was about to start.

"This *is* the London train?" Oz asked a rather startled woman, waving farewell from a window.

"Just you stay there, my lad," said a railway inspector, shouting at him from across the track. "We've had enough of hooligans like you."

Oz revved up the engine and roared along the platform, knocking over piles of luggage and setting free several trolleys which began to roll along the platform.

The train set off slowly, but Oz quickly caught it up, thanks to his super Suzuki GS 1000.

At the back of the train, a guard was leaning out of the window. As Oz roared alongside, he shoved the parcel into the guard's hand.

"Here you are, mate," said the Oz. "For the PM, personal. To be picked up at Euston. Keep it safe. Cheers."

As Oz handed over the parcel, he found he had come to the end of the platform. Oz nearly fell off, but he managed to brake just in time. Then he and the giant bike slithered down a ramp and skidded into some cinders beside the track. There was a lot of crackling and screeching from the radio at the back of his bike, but Oz ignored it.

"That was lucky," he said, putting the bike straight and dusting the cinders from his clothes. "I don't think I would have liked to ride all the way to London on the railway track. Would have been a bit bumpy. And a bit hairy . . ."

Over his shoulder, he could see and hear various railway officials yelling at him to come back.

To his left were some coal heaps in a sort of coal marshalling yard. Oz turned the bike and roared into the yard, then out of a gate at the other side.

"Another job well done," said Oz. "I bet I'm the best messenger boy they ever had."

On the way back to his estate, Oz slowed down slightly, as he was of course in a built-up area, with a 30 mph speed limit. He was now so confident that he was trying a few extra tricks, such as standing up as he rode the bike.

He noticed a familiar figure walking along the pavement, a rather fat, tubby, serious-looking girl with spectacles.

"Wanna lift?" he said to her.

It was Flossie Teacake.

"I don't take lifts from strangers."

"How can I be a stranger," said Oz, "when I know you're called Flossie Teacake and you're in Miss Turkey's class at school and you've a brother and sister and you live near a very clever, very strong, very intelligent boy called Ossie Osgood."

Flossie stopped in amazement. "How do you know all that?"

"Jump on," said Oz. "I'll drop you off at your house. I know a short cut down this lane. I won't go too fast."

So Flossie got on. Oz deliberately made as much noise as he could, revving up the engine. Flossie held on tightly, her arms round Oz.

The ride to her home only took a few minutes and then she was in no hurry to get off.

"God, it's an amazing bike," she said, climbing down. "And you ride it so well."

"Easy, when you know how," said Oz.

Her father had been digging in the front garden as they roared up. "What are you doing on that bike, Flossie? You haven't even got a crash helmet on. Whose is it anyway . . ."

"Got to rush," said Oz. "More emergency parcels to deliver. I dunno. Some of these dads are so stupid . . ."

Oz left the motorbike outside the pub, just where he had found it. The real rider still seemed to be inside. Oz thought about telling him what he had done.

"I've probably saved his job, doing that emergency delivery for him."

But he decided against it. It was now almost one o'clock. Oz would have to get home in time for lunch, or his mother would wonder where he was. But first he had to change back to Ossie again. If he could. He only hoped that going back into the wardrobe would do the trick.

He took off the helmet, hooked it over the radio aerial, then went into his grandfather's block, letting himself in with his own key . . .

Very quietly and carefully, walking on tiptoe, he listened for his grandfather. He could hear the television still blaring away. He slipped into the bedroom, went over to the wardrobe and stepped inside, letting the door close gently behind him. He felt for the Iron Cross and the other objects, wondering if it would work, if the magic would operate in reverse.

He now wanted to be eleven years old once again, so he stood there, his eyes closed, his hands clenched, wishing and wishing, till he felt his body beginning to tremble.

When he stepped out, he was Ossie again.

*

"What have you got up your jumper?" said his mother as Ossie came into the house, leaving his BMX in the hall.

"Nothing, Mum."

"Don't be silly, I saw the bulge."

"Just comics. That's all. Grandad gave me some money for doing his shopping, so I bought some new ones."

"As if you haven't got enough."

"I can never get enough comics," said Ossie.

"I hope you haven't been riding your bike carrying all those comics like that."

"Course not," said Ossie. "I never do dangerous things on bikes. What's for lunch? I'm starving . . ."

3

Ossie the Strong Man

Miss Turkey, Ossie's form teacher, told the class that she would have to leave them five minutes early. There was something she had to do in the staff room. She wanted them to be quiet; then when the bell rang, they had to go out to play in an orderly fashion. Was that clear?

"Right," said Flossie, the moment the classroom door was closed. "You are the last one left."

Ossie was sitting at his table, which he shared with six other boys and girls, trying to do some Maths, at least thinking about doing some Maths, looking at his SMILE work card but unable to understand what he was supposed to do.

"Ouch, gerroff," shouted Ossie.

His arm had been grabbed by Flossie. She was sitting on his left while Desmond was on his right.

"Come on," said Flossie. "It's your turn."

"I don't need your rotten help," said Ossie. "I can do these stupid cards on my own."

"Put your arm straight," said Flossie. "Don't cheat."

Flossie had rolled up her ample sleeve, to reveal her ample arm. There were no actual muscles, but masses of solid fat.

"All I've got is masses of solid thin," thought Ossie, resigned to the inevitable, slowly rolling up his jumper to expose his matchstick arm.

He had not realized at first that it was arm wrestling. All that week, Flossie had taken on and beaten every boy and girl in their class. So far, Ossie had escaped her notice.

It had been the same at primary school. At least six girls in Ossie's class had been bigger and stronger, as well as cleverer, than Ossie. He had thought at secondary school things would change. His mother had promised him a spurt, whatever that was. Perhaps she would get him a spurt for Christmas.

"Right," said Dez, being bossy. "I'll time you."

Dez took off his watch and said he would give them ten seconds using their right arms, then ten seconds using their left arms.

"I've got a broken arm," said Ossie. "This one 'ere. Oh, it's agony. And me left arm has got a virus and the doctor said I hadn't to use it till they do an X-ray at the hospital . . ."

"They'd need a microscope, not an X-ray on your arm," said Flossie. "Just to find it."

In five seconds, she had forced his right arm flat. They changed to left arms, and that took only two seconds.

"There, I told you," said Ossie. "That's my virus arm. I just let you win, Flossie Teacake. I just let you win both . . ."

Ossie trailed off his sentence, rather mournfully. Flossie by this time had gone back to her SMILE card, finishing another problem with absolute ease.

Then the bell went, and Miss Turkey's class quietly went out to play.

"Fight! Fight! Fight!"

The chant soon went up right round the playground. Children miles away, getting on with their own little games, or standing talking to each other, or in some cases just standing, they stopped whatever they had been doing and they all started rushing across the playground, drawn by those exciting words.

"Fight! Fight! Fight!"

Boys as well as girls were pushing and shoving, trying to get the best view, all laughing and cheering, though not quite sure who or what or why they were laughing and cheering. It was being part of the crowd that was good fun. In a playground fight the onlookers have a part to play, all actors in the same show.

Ossie was in the bike sheds, swapping some *Beanos* with Dez. They were making so much noise, squabbling over prices, arguing over who owned which, that at first they didn't realize a fight had started at the far end of the playground.

"Just ignore it," said Ossie. "Come on, I'll swap you two new *Eagles* for that old *Dandy*."

"Yeah," said Dez. "'Member last week it was all over by the time we got there."

"That wasn't a fight anyway," said Ossie. "Just some stupid second-year girls pretending there was a fight, just to get us running."

"No, it wasn't," said Dez. "It was a real bundle.

It was that third-year kid Hawkins. I saw him in the afternoon wif a bleeding nose. It was a really good fight."

A group of sixth formers, all of them enormous, some even with moustaches, raced past, leaving their football game in the Big Playground.

Younger kids were never allowed near this stretch, or they got thumped. Usually, sixth formers carried on playing whenever there was a fight. They had seen it all. Just another silly fight. Who cares. Pass the ball.

"Come on, let's go," said Ossie. "It must be a mass fight."

He and Dez grabbed their comics from the ground, shoving them inside their parkers.

It looked to Ossie as though Dez had picked up some of Ossie's comics, but perhaps he had just imagined it. They were both in such a rush.

"Fight! Fight! Fight!" they both shouted as they ran across the playground, pushing each other and making angry faces, holding up their clenched fists, as if they themselves were in a fight.

That's what you did, even if you were just watching. You pretended to be lashing out at all your friends, just as a giggle, grabbing arms as if you were going to break them, squaring up jaw to jaw, then you burst out laughing and stopped.

Ossie and Dez wormed their way through the legs and under the bodies. That was about the only advantage of being small and weedy, thought Ossie. In a big crowd, you could always edge in, though you stood a chance of someone accidentally standing on you, or deliberately kicking you, or either accidentally or deliberately bashing you on the head with their plastic carrier bags.

Ossie had arrived at school on his first day with a brand new leather briefcase which his mother had bought him.

Now, he was trying as hard as possible to ruin it, to make it as scruffy and worn as possible. His mother insisted each day he had to take it, much to his fury. The older forms usually carried their things in sports bags. But the sixth form, the giants at the top of the school, they all carried plastic carrier bags, the sort you get at supermarkets. Ossie could not quite work this out, but he had already felt a few of the bags round his ear and knew they could be quite dangerous, if you happened to get in the way.

"Wish I was bigger," thought Ossie. "When you're big, then other kids *have* to get out of your way. Or you make them. Must be really good, being eighteen and in the sixth form."

Ossie and Dez were working their way so quickly through the crowd, crawling on their hands and knees, that they must have lost their sense of direction, or been pushed the wrong way. They suddenly found themselves catapulted into fresh air again. That at least was some small relief.

"What a pong in there," said Ossie. "Did you smell all those trainers?"

"I thought it was you," said Dez.

Ossie gave him a punch, then they both turned round and pushed back into the throng, hoping this time to find a way to the epicentre of the little earthquake known as a playground fight.

"Hope it's fourth years," said Ossie.

"Yeh," said Dez. "They're the hard men, the fourth years."

"Must be," said Ossie. "Be over by now, if it was

just first years. I hope it's that punky one, with the orange hair."

"Or that headbanger in the leather, the one who stands at the front gate."

Ossie was rather frightened by both of these boys and made a point of never going through the front gate if he saw them around. They usually did stand there, all the hard men, waiting for the girls.

"Boo! Boo! Boo!"

The shouts of "Fight! Fight! Fight!" had suddenly turned to booing, just as Ossie and Dez had finally worked their way to the middle of the circle and were within touching distance of the actual combatants.

Ossie was sure he could see real blood on the ground, but at that moment the crowd began to collapse, people backed away, the two fighters were picking up their things, wiping their clothes, feeling their bruises.

"Boo! Boo! Boo!"

Three teachers had arrived and were quickly breaking up the crowds, grabbing several kids by the scruff of their collars and hauling them forcibly out of the way.

Ossie recognized one of them as Mr Bott, a PE teacher he didn't like. He also noticed that it was the smaller kids they were pulling out of the way, not any of the hard men from the fourth years.

"Boo! Boo! Boo!" shouted Ossie and Dez at the teachers, though from a distance, careful not to be seen.

It was quite fun, after a fight was over, when everyone joined in shouting "Boo! Boo! Boo!"

Not quite as good, though, as shouting "Fight! Fight! Fight!"

"That was your fault, Ossie," said Dez.

They were back in the bike sheds, getting out their comics again.

"Rubbish," said Ossie.

"If you had gone when I said, we would of seen that fight."

"Get lost," said Ossie.

"You was scared anyway. You was scared of the fight. I seen you."

Dez was only an inch taller than Ossie, but he was rather better built. Almost anyone in the whole world, Ossie thought, was better built than he was.

"Anyways," said Ossie, "that's my comic. You pinched it. I saw you."

"No, I didn't," said Dez. "It's mine."

"Liar."

Ossie grabbed it and pointed to the pencil mark in the top right-hand corner.

"Look, number sixty-nine. That's my number. See. Proves it."

"So what," said Dez. "I live at sixty-nine as well."

"No, you don't."

"Yes, I do."

"No, you don't."

"Prove it."

Ossie had never been to Dez's house. Dez lived in a big block of flats, but Ossie wasn't sure where. He had been to nobody's house so far, nor had anyone from his new school come to his house.

There was silence for a while, as Ossie angrily picked up the comics that were his, the ones Dez agreed belonged to him, but he was still convinced Dez had taken three which were really his property.

"You get on my bleeding nerves," said Ossie.

"Get lost," said Dez.

Ossie was standing up slowly, as if going away, then he suddenly bent down and tried to grab the three comics. Dez was just as quick and held Ossie by the arm.

"Wanna fight, eh," said Dez.

"I just want my comics," said Ossie. "Thief."

"Right, that's it," said Dez. "You asked for it."

"Oh, get lost," said Ossie.

Ossie didn't want a fight. He had never had one in all his primary school years, and hoped he never would.

With his physique, there was really no point.

"Fight! Fight! Fight!"

Once again, the shout went round the playground, though this time the roars and noise were not quite so deep or intense. Most people realized the fight was in the bike sheds. That was where the little kids, the first years, usually congregated, out of the way of the big lads. All the same, there were soon enough people shouting. A fight, after all, was a fight.

Ossie and Dez had taken their parkers off. Ossie wasn't sure why, but as Dez had done so, he was

forced to do the same.

Several bigger kids had appeared on the scene, as if from nowhere, and had quickly taken over Ossie's and Dez's coats and were urging them on, pushing them against each other.

Ossie could already feel his asthma coming on. It

usually did if he got over-excited, but as he held up his fists and tightened his muscles, which made no difference to their size but did make the muscles *feel* tighter, his spirit at least felt slightly stronger, even if his body was not.

He could sense Dez backing off. Perhaps he looked quite fearsome, now that there was no retreat. He was willing himself to be strong, even if physically he could never manage it. He knew from experience, when he had rows with Lucy, that if you *looked* fierce, as if you meant it, that was the battle half won.

They moved round in circles for a while, each keeping their distance. The crowd was yelling them on, though a lot were laughing and jeering, making fun of little Ossie.

"I'd rather watch girls fighting," said two fourth years, moving away again.

Dez gave a quick punch. It was not a particularly hard one, almost a shadow punch, but it caught Ossie in the pit of his stomach. He thought he was going to stop breathing and his body seemed to double up.

He could sense Dez coming in again, so he

grabbed hold of him like a frightened cat and held on, digging his nails into Dez's neck, yelling and shouting, pinning him with his arms so that Dez couldn't hit him any more.

"Boo! Boo! Boo!"

The teachers arrived very quickly as there had been no time to return to the staff room. The fight had only lasted thirty seconds, though to Ossie it had seemed like hours.

"I won," said Ossie, staggering away, blood coming from his nose.

"I won," said Dez, holding his neck as if it had been broken.

Ossie felt rotten for the rest of the morning at school, but not rotten enough to go home. He knew his mother would be at work all morning. Not much fun coming home with tales of woe if there was nobody to tell them to.

But after school dinner he went to see the school nurse, displayed his bruises, managed a few asthmatic wheezes, and was sent home.

"Right," said his mother, drawing the curtains. "I

want you to have a nice sleep this afternoon."

"Can I have a drink?" said Ossie. "Any Coke?"

"Certainly not," said his mother. "Someone too ill for school is too ill to drink Coke."

"My comics," said Ossie, giving another wheeze. "Put them near, just in case I don't sleep."

"Just you try to sleep first," said his mother. "I'll make sure Lucy doesn't disturb you when she comes home, then we'll all have a nice supper together. If you're feeling better."

It was lucky having his mother doing only a part-time job, though now and again she was called in to do afternoons as well, if there were emergencies. She taught at the primary school Ossie used to go to. She was a Point Five teacher. Ossie used to think it meant that only half of her went to school each day. That was when he was little. Even littler than he was now.

"I'll pop round to the shop and get you some new comics," she said. "But I won't give you them till this evening. If you feel up to it."

"Thanks, Mum," said Ossie.

He might scream at her, call her a stupid old woman, but now and again mothers did have their uses, when you felt rotten.

Ossie woke up. He looked at his digital watch, pressing the button to light it, but it didn't work. Stupid watch.

He felt as if he had been asleep for hours, though his head was a bit sore, and so were his arms. He pulled his arms out of the blankets carefully. They looked even smaller and more fragile than ever.

"If only I could trade them in for a better pair," he thought.

With computers and videos, bikes and training shoes, there were new and improved models coming out every year, sometimes every month, or so it seemed.

"They should do that with arms," thought Ossie. "And legs. Fact, I could do with a completely new body. Fed up with this old skinny one. That would be a really good special offer for the soap packets. Who wants those stupid old rail tickets."

Ossie loved all special offers, free trials and competitions. He had beside his bed a little pile of rail vouchers, which he had carefully sent for and collected. But never used. Ossie never went anywhere.

One of these days he would be ready, with his free rail tickets, to go right round the world.

"But I know what'll happen. They'll have changed the rules by then. Or given up using trains."

His eyes had become more used to the semi-dark and he picked up his watch again. It was ten past two. He had slept for only ten minutes.

"When I was on that motorbike," he thought to himself, "I had huge arms then. And a huge body. And huge legs. But you do, when you're grown up. That was really excellent."

Ossie lay back, thinking hard. Had he just imagined it? Could it *really* have happened? What sort of magic had been in the wardrobe that day to make the strange transformation?

"I bet it'll never happen again. Just my bad luck. Not much point trying anyway. Not with this rotten wheezy chest."

Ossie tried a few of his special breathing exercises, ones he had made up for himself, when he tried to talk himself into thinking he was better, and it did seem as if his asthma was beginning to disappear.

"Afternoon school will just be starting," thought Ossie. "What am I going to do here? It's so boring lying in bed."

His asthma had now gone. At least for a while. When he really was eighteen, so his mother had promised him, then it would go completely. He would grow out of it, so she said.

"At eighteen, it seems to me I'll grow out of *everything*. This rotten body, this wheezy chest. I'll grow into somebody new. So they all say. I don't really believe it will ever happen."

He looked at his watch. It was now twelve minutes past two.

"I know, I'll go and see Grandad . . ."

Ossie could hear his grandad snoring in the next room, sitting in his armchair, having his afternoon rest. The television was still on, but very low.

He gently went into the bedroom, climbed over all Grandad's treasures and opened the wardrobe.

Very slowly Ossie stepped inside, letting the door swing back behind him. At once, he was in a strange world where there seemed to be no time and only infinite space.

Ossie closed his eyes and wished and wished that he could be grown up now, an eighteen-year-old, big enough and old enough to be in the sixth form.

He stepped out of the wardrobe, wondering if it would still work. His body had seemed to shake and shiver, but he wasn't sure if he had just imagined it. Something mysterious had happened the first time, but would it always be the same?

He looked at himself in the mirror. There was Oz. So tall and strong, so different in so many ways, but in his eyes he could see his real self, smiling knowingly.

In the mirror, he noticed a sort of darkness on his upper lip. He felt it carefully. It was rather feathery, almost hairy. What on earth could it be?

"Don't say I'll have to start shaving, just 'cos I've become eighteen. Oh, what a drag . . ."

Oz ran all the way to school. He could see sights which were normally hidden from him. Now that he was six foot, he could look over walls and over hedges, straight into people's lives.

He saw dads who worked night shifts, or who had no work at all, sitting slumped in armchairs, green

shadows flickering on the walls behind them, showing they were lost in afternoon television. He saw
fourth-year boys he knew should be at school,
playing snooker and smoking with their friends. He
heard fourth-year girls, who should also have been
at school, sitting in upstairs bedrooms, the windows
wide open, playing very loud pop music and shouting rude remarks at each other.

He saw silhouettes of silent mothers, sitting at
polished dining tables. Beside them, in their high
chairs, were fat babies, having their afternoon
feeds. Even without stretching, Oz could almost
taste the spoonfuls of sticky, gooey food going off
in the direction of each high chair.

"I'm glad I'm not eating that baby muck,"
thought Oz. "Or even any eleven-year-old muck. I
wonder what muck eighteen-year-olds eat?"

Oz ran faster and faster, which was quite easy,
without at all getting out of breath. He had on very
tight but faded Levi jeans, expensive Nike training
shoes and a grey Benetton top, just like any normal
sixth former.

When you become eighteen, however suddenly,
you must always dress the part.

"Hi," said Oz very cheerfully to several sixth-form boys and girls as he passed them in the corridor.

Only one said "Hi" back. The rest grunted. Oz made a mental note to grunt from now on.

He was looking for the sixth-form common room, the room especially reserved for sixth-form boys and girls. He had never been in it before.

Normally, he would be frightened just to meet them in the corridors. It was impossible to tell which were sixth formers and which were staff. The staff, on the whole, wore scruffier and older clothes. That was about the only difference.

He hesitated at the door. Two girls came up behind him, pushed ahead and went in. He had noticed this about sixth-form girls. They never waited for anyone or anything. They just went right ahead. And if you gave them cheek, as he and Dez sometimes did, they would often run after you and belt you.

"Just what we want," said one girl with pink hair as soon as Oz entered the room.

"What?" said Oz.

He was looking around, wondering who she was talking to.

"We've got to move this stuff for the disco. Give us a hand, will you? We're knackered."

Oz was about to walk out again. Two girls were struggling with three or four battered couches and chairs which they were trying to move to the side of the room.

With one hand, he gave the smallest armchair a gentle push, and at once it slid right across the floor. He could hardly believe his eyes. Perhaps it had wheels. He then bodily picked up a couch, just like that, and carried it all the way to the wall.

In just a few minutes he had moved every piece of furniture so that the middle of the room was completely clear. He then moved a heavy table from the end of the room to the doorway. The girls said they wanted it there so they could collect the tickets.

"My hero," they all said. "Which tutor group are you in?"

"Miss Turkey's," said Oz, without thinking.

"I thought she only took first years," said one of the girls.

"Actually, I take them," said Oz. "But don't tell everyone."

"Are you in my Maths set?" said another girl,

looking at him carefully. "You do look familiar."

"Gotta go now," said Oz, moving to the door.

"You will come to the disco, won't you?" said a girl.

"Yes," said another. "We need some hunky men tonight."

As he left the common room, Oz could still hear them laughing.

"I didn't know eighteen-year-old boys could cause such amusement," thought Oz, rather pleased with himself.

There were sounds of angry shouting as Oz walked past the school swimming pool. He looked in and saw that Mr Bott, head of PE, was taking a class. As usual, he was being horrid to all the little first years, banging them on the head with a huge pole which he used whenever they did anything wrong.

"I wish I could swim properly," thought Oz. "Must be really good."

As an eleven-year-old, he had been excused swimming. His mother gave him a note every week, saying he had asthma. His breathing was not up to it. But this was partly because he was scared of being hit over the head with Mr Bott's pole.

Mr Bott was screaming at some girl who was resting at the far end, telling her to hurry up and do another length. He was shouting so much that he slipped and only just managed to stop himself falling into the water. Oz burst out laughing.

"What are you grinning at, boy?" shouted Mr Bott.

"Nothing, sir," said Oz, beginning to quake like a little first year. Then he realized that as a huge six footer, a massive sixth former, now taller than old Botty, he had no need to be scared.

"If you're so clever," shouted Mr Bott, "get undressed and show these ignoramuses how to swim."

"Fine," said Oz, surprised at his own voice, not just its depth but his confidence. "No problem."

Botty threw him a spare costume and Oz quickly went into a cubicle and got undressed.

A few moments later, Oz stood at the far end, ready to dive. But would he be able to swim? Oz suddenly had a few doubts.

"Come on, laddie," shouted Botty. "I thought you were going to let this shower see how it's done."

Oz paused for a few moments, then he closed his eyes and dived.

All the first years stopped practising in order to watch. So did Mr Bott, leaning right over the pool, ready to criticize.

There was no sign of Oz. He seemed to have disappeared. Mr Bott stared harder into the deep end, wondering if this sixth former, whom he hadn't quite recognized anyway, had hit his head by doing such a flash racing dive at the shallow end.

Suddenly Oz emerged, having swum the whole length of the bath under water, an amazing feat, which few people in the whole school could ever hope to match. He threw his arms up in the air, catching Mr Bott by surprise, and completely soaked him. This time, Mr Bott did slip, falling straight into the pool. His track suit immediately filled with water and he sank.

"Now children," said Oz. "This is a very good example of life-saving. Jolly kind of Mr Bott to help us in this demonstration. Watch carefully and I'm sure you will all get your bronze medals."

Oz took the long pole from the side of the pool and hooked Mr Bott with it, grabbing him by the

back of his track-suit top. Then lying on his back, holding the pole, Oz did a magnificent back crawl right up the pool, dragging Mr Bott behind him.

The whole class cheered. Oz felt so strong and powerful. He felt he could have done twenty lengths, and very quickly, but he didn't want to go too fast. Mr Bott did seem to be struggling a lot.

At the deep end, Oz unhooked him and then helped him out of the water. Mr Bott lay on the side, choking and spluttering.

"No, don't thank me," said Oz, as he went to get changed. "No problem. By the way, Mr Bott, have you ever thought of taking up synchronized swimming?"

Oz thought he would just have a quick look in his own class room, form 1M, to see what was happening, though he wondered what he might say to Miss Turkey. Would she recognize him, he wondered?

He opened the door slowly, but she wasn't there. At once all the class started yelling at him.

"You a prefect?" said Desmond.

"You come to take us, sir?" said Flossie.

"You a teacher?" said another girl.

"No, he ain't," said Desmond. "He's just a stupid sixth former. I know him."

"Please sit down, everyone," said Oz, going to Miss Turkey's desk.

"We always stand up," said Desmond. "Miss says we can stand up if we like."

"I said sit down," said Oz.

"I know your face," said Desmond.

"I always wear it," said Oz. "That's why you know it. Now sit down. I think we'll do Maths this afternoon, really hard stuff."

"Oh, no," said Desmond. "Not boring old Maths."

Desmond and another boy were still standing at the front, very cheeky and defiant.

Oz looked at them carefully. Then in one movement he pounced and grabbed each one by the back of his jumper before they realized what had happened. Oz hoisted them clean off the ground and held them up in the air. He carried them across the classroom and then, from quite a height, he dropped each of them in his place.

They had both been yelling and moaning while being carried, but the breath was knocked out of them as they landed. They slumped in their chairs, holding their bottoms. This time, they were very quiet indeed.

"Thank you very much," said Miss Turkey coming into the room. "I got detained in the staff room. Very kind of you."

"A pleasure," said Oz. "They were playing up a bit when I passed, but I soon settled them."

"Yes, one or two of them are rather unruly. Are you Upper Sixth or Lower Sixth?"

"Eh, sort of Middling Sixth," said Oz.

"Have you got a younger brother in the first year?" she asked. "You do look familiar."

"Yeh, but he's very small," said Oz, going out of the door. "You probably have never noticed him. Small and quiet . . ."

Oz was going down the library corridor when a sixth-form girl stepped out of the library and took him by the hand.

"Come on, you can be the judge," she said, dragging him in.

Two girls were sitting at a table in a far corner, almost hidden by the bookshelves, silently locked in an arm wrestle.

"Big girls like them," said Oz, "playing first-year games? I gave that up in primary school. Kids' stuff."

The girl motioned to him to keep quiet, putting her finger to her lips. In the library, as Oz well knew, it was supposed to be quiet study.

He followed her to the table and just as he got there, the smaller of the two girls stood up in triumph, holding her hands above her head in a victorious salute. She had obviously won the contest, even before Oz could judge it. The other girl had conceded defeat.

"What about him, Fanny," said the girl who had brought Oz into the library. "I bet you can't beat him."

"How much do you bet?" said Fanny.

"Bet you a pound you can't," said the girl.

Oz started to mutter excuses. He didn't really want to wrestle with a girl. He was a huge, eighteen-year-old boy. It wouldn't seem fair.

"Eh, I haven't time, really," began Oz. "My mum expects me home and anyway I should really be in bed and . . ."

"Scared, are you," said Fanny, pulling him into the chair opposite her. "Left or right arm?"

She took Oz's right hand in her right hand and then straightened their arms, measuring with her eye to make sure they were each at right angles to the desk.

"That's a nasty spot you've got on your neck," she said, staring into Oz's face.

Oz felt his neck with his left hand. He must have picked up a little scratch, perhaps in the gym, when he had been fooling around, or with carrying Desmond. As he carefully moved his hand along his neck, he felt a definite spot, and then another, a row of three little spots he had not seen before.

"Considering your age," said Fanny, "you haven't got many spots."

"What?" said Oz.

"Oh, do stop fussing," said Fanny.

She suddenly pressed down with all her might and Oz, to his amazement, felt his arm giving way. He had only been half concentrating on the contest, but even so, she had proved to be remarkably strong.

"Even at eighteen," he said, getting up, "I get

beaten by a girl."

"Nothing wrong with that," said Fanny.

"I didn't mean it like that," he said smiling. He was surprised to find he wasn't at all upset.

"Pure technique," said Fanny, taking a pound coin from her friend. "That's all it is."

The bell went and everyone in the library got up and started to pack their books in their bags.

"That was quite good fun," thought Oz. "When you're big and strong, eighteen and grown-up, it obviously doesn't matter so much being beaten. Well, now and again. You can take it, when you're eighteen."

Oz looked at his watch and realized he would have to run to get to his grandad's, and then home before Lucy got back.

"Funny about the spots, though. That's something I hadn't expected about being eighteen. Perhaps it isn't all fun . . ."

"Have some more noodles," said Mrs Osgood, going to the stove. "You have made a miracle recovery."

"Well, I'm not quite perfect yet," said Ossie. "So

you can all be kind to me a bit longer. And that means you, Lucy."

"Yes, your majesty," said Lucy.

"And I've made some apple crumble for afters," said Mrs Osgood. "If you think you are *really* better now."

"Sort of," said Ossie. "But keep your voices low. People shouting gets on my nerves."

Lucy and Mrs Osgood smiled at each other, but without letting Ossie see.

"You look OK to me now, Ossie," said Lucy.

"Well, I had a very quiet afternoon, all on my own."

"Do you want me to go up to that school?" said his mother. "I could speak to the Head Master."

"Don't worry, Mum," said Ossie. "It was just a bit of pushing, not a proper fight. Anyway, I bet Desmond feels worse than me now. I did drop him a long way."

"Drop him?" said his mother.

"Yeh, technical term, in boxing," said Ossie. "You sort of drop a punch on him."

"What's happened to your face, Ossie?" said Lucy.

"Nothing," said Ossie. "What's wrong with it?"

"You've got spots," she said, leaning forward and staring at his neck.

"Don't be silly," said his mother. "He's only eleven. Boys don't get spots till, well, they're much older. Now get on with your tea, Lucy."

When they were all busy eating again, Ossie carefully felt his face, just to make sure. There were some marks there, very tender as well.

Could they be real spots? Starting already? Or just some small bruises from the playground fight with Desmond?

"Perhaps I will have some of that apple crumble, Mum. I need to keep up my strength . . ."

4

Ossie Goes to Spurs

Ossie was standing in the corridor watching the notice board. He had been hanging around for some time because he knew that the first-year football team was due to be put up.

When Miss Headache emerged from her little office Ossie rushed forward, only to be knocked over by about ten other first years, all of whom, purely by chance, had just been hanging around.

"She's made a mistake," said Ossie. "I've been missed off."

"You're useless," said Desmond, "that's why you've been missed off."

"It's victimization," said Ossie. "She's never liked me, that stupid woman. I'm complaining to the School Council. She should never have been the referee in the trial. Stands to reason. Having a stupid woman refereeing a football match, what do you expect."

"Well she chose me," said Desmond, "so she must be good."

"I was ill that day," said Ossie. "That was the problem. Otherwise she would have seen how good I am."

Ossie considered himself a very good player, skilful, full of little tricks, marvellous at dribbling. It was only his lack of height and strength which stopped the rest of the world from knowing this. That and his asthma. Very often, he could hardly run because of being so quickly out of breath. And even when he kicked with all his might, the ball hardly went any distance at all.

"If she'd seen me on form," said Ossie, "I would probably have been made captain by now."

As it was, Craig had been made captain. He was quite a good player. Ossie admitted that. Dez was vice captain. That was ridiculous. Ossie considered he was just as good as Dez.

He took another look at the board. Still no sign of his name. Not even as a reserve.

"Diabolical," said Ossie. "Who wants to play in their rotten team anyway? I've got better things to do on Saturdays."

"Stand aside fans," said Craig. He had just seen the notice board and his head, so Ossie thought, was already twice as big.

"Autographs later," said Craig. "No time now, folks. Out of the way, peasants."

Ossie was furious. He didn't mind people being good at things, but he hated them showing off. He agreed with his grandfather.

"What a big head," shouted Ossie, going off quickly down the corridor.

Craig ran after him, but Ossie was already into the playground where he had caught up with Flossie. Craig might be captain of the first-year team, but he too was quite small and weedy. One glare from Flossie was enough to put Craig, or any other boy, in his place.

"Any shopping wanted, Grandad?" said Ossie.

"Where have you been, my lad?" shouted Grandad from his living room. "Been hours waiting for you."

Ossie dropped his school bag in the hall. The bag was becoming quite beat-up by now, looking decidedly old and worn. Throwing it around the playground at Dez had done it a lot of good.

Ossie went into the living room and was amazed to find his grandad standing on a chair fixing a coat hanger to the picture rail.

"Decorating, Grandad? I thought you'd just painted this room."

"It's for you, boyo. Here, stand on this chair and hold on to this."

Ossie did as he was told, and immediately the wire coat hanger began to bend. Grandad then got two other wire hangers, and fixed all three together.

Ossie held on, his feet just a few centimetres off the ground. This time, the coat hanger held his weight.

"Right, every day after school I want you to spend ten minutes doing these exercises. We'll soon get you up to six feet. We'll soon have you with big arm muscles. No problems."

"I'm tired, Grandad," said Ossie, hanging on grimly.

"Don't you dare move. You'll get the back of my hand."

"I want the lavatory."

"You'll have to want."

"Can I have a drink?"

"Not till you've done ten minutes. When I was your age, I used to hang from the banisters every evening. That's how I got to be big and strong."

"But you're not big and strong, Grandad."

"Less of your cheek, my lad."

"Oh, Grandad. I'm going to faint. I can't hang on. My hands are killing me. I'm going to let go . . ."

And with that, Ossie fell off the coat hanger. As he was only just slightly off the ground, he didn't have far to go.

"Look at my hands," said Ossie. "Look at the marks. I won't be able to do my homework now. I'm telling Mum. All your fault."

"Tomorrow night," said Grandad, "I'll try it with a bit of padding. Perhaps some rubber will give you a better hold."

"Oh, no, Grandad, it won't work. I'll never be tall."

"Stand still a minute. Look at me. Head up, boyo. Yes, I really do think you've put on half an inch. It's working already. See, I told you."

*

Grandad had switched on children's TV, which he never missed, so Ossie went into the bedroom to have a quick look around. Just to cheer himself up. There was nothing really specific he wanted, no one special wish he wanted granted, apart from the usual things, all ten million of them.

"Just looking at your treasures, Grandad," shouted Ossie, putting the light on so he could see properly.

Underneath Grandad's bed, Ossie noticed an open box of postcards, which Grandad had been given for his birthday, specially printed with his name and address.

"I knew it was stupid," thought Oz. "I told Mum he would never use them. Who does he write to, at his age? Daft."

Ossie was just about to leave the bedroom, because he knew his mother was expecting him home, when it struck him that perhaps he could use one of his grandad's postcards. They did look very impressive, with his name and address all nicely printed. Very official.

Ossie took his best school felt pen out of his school bag, and started writing.

Dear Spurs. You must of herd about Ossie Osgood cos he is a veree good plare and I rely fink he shood be playing for Spurs so plase will you give him a trile. Tak no notis of that stoopid Miss Headache cos she nose nuffink about footbal. Yours sinserly.
Oswald Osgood.

Ossie sat and admired his handiwork. The hand-writing was quite good, neat and well formed, for a fairly average sort of eleven-year-old. But Ossie realized the spelling was perhaps not as good as it might be. Very eleven-year-old in fact.

He looked on his grandad's shelves and found a dictionary. Then, by a great stroke of luck, he found an old typewriter. "If only I knew how to use it."

At Ossie's school they did Commercial Studies in the fourth year, both boys and girls, but that was years ahead. If only he was eighteen now.

Ossie listened carefully. His grandfather was still occupied with the television: he could hear him shouting out comments. He turned the bedroom light off, to help the atmosphere, then he opened the big wardrobe and stepped inside.

The wardrobe smelled even more of mothballs than it had the last time he had been there. And it felt even darker and creepier. Had he perhaps stepped inside too quickly? It had all been a bit sudden. Ossie closed his eyes, and wished very hard, but quite quickly this time; he only wished for a little wish.

When he opened the door, it had happened again. He was now Oz. Aged eighteen.

It was an old typewriter, a Remington, but the ribbon was almost new and once he had dusted and cleaned it, Oz quickly typed out a neat message on one of Grandad's postcards. His typing was quite good, but of course at eighteen, after two years of Commercial Studies, it should be.

This time he kept the wording simple and stuck to the facts.

> Ossie Osgood is the star of his school team. He is eighteen, over six feet high. He is a very good player.

"Well," thought Oz, "that's true. I have always been a very good player. At eighteen, I am *bound* to be the star of that stupid school team."

> I would like you to give him a trial.
> P.S. Arsenal are sending someone to see him tomorrow. But he wants to play for Spurs.

Oz thought that PS was a master stroke. That would really get them excited.

He was still not sure how to spell "sincerely", despite being eighteen. That page had been torn out of the dictionary. In the end he got round the problem and signed the postcard with a flourish.

> Yours in Sport, Oswald Osgood, Senior.

Then he went back into the wardrobe, quickly touched in turn the cavalry boots and the shrapnel, finishing with the Iron Cross. He opened his eyes and came out again. Then he went home, taking the card with him.

He found a first-class stamp in the box on the hall shelf, where his mother always kept the stamps, and posted the card next day on the way to school. Then he forgot all about it.

It was Saturday morning, two weeks later, and

Ossie was getting his breakfast. This was the new rule. His mother had decided that from now on Ossie and Lucy should look after themselves at weekends. They were both old enough by now.

Ossie was furious with Lucy, who as usual had been first up. She had finished all the Cocoa Pops. These were Ossie's favourite for this week. It meant he had to have Weetabix instead.

"Mum," shouted Lucy, "he's taking all the milk."

"Well, she's taken all the Cocoa Pops."

"If you got up earlier in the morning," said Lucy, "you could have had them. There was only enough for one."

Ossie had fallen silent. There was a new competition on the back of the cereal packet. For just one pound you could join a club and get something or other. He might earn that pound today, after he had done his grandad's shopping.

"Mum, I hope you've done them," Ossie shouted suddenly. "Oh God, woman, sometimes you are just so stupid."

"You two are not still arguing over the cereal

packets, are you?" said Mother, coming into the room. "You are a pain, Ossie Osgood."

"No," moaned Ossie. "It's my jeans. I put them out for you in the dirty laundry basket. I told you days ago. I want to wear them today. I'm going to watch the school team."

"Oh," said Lucy, smirking. "Little Ossie wants to wear his best jeans. Are you going to the match with Flossie?"

Ossie gave her a push.

"What have you been doing all week anyway?" said Ossie. "One pair of jeans. Not much work in that. You've got a washing machine, haven't you? That's what they're for, washing things."

"Is Flossie your girlfriend then, Ossie?" said Lucy.

"I'm going with Desmond, so that's got you."

This time he pushed her so hard she fell off her chair. She pretended to cry, but when she realized her mother had gone upstairs, she soon stopped.

"Why are you going to watch the team?" said Lucy. "I thought *you* would be *in* the team. Always telling us how good you are."

"Get lost," said Ossie.

Mrs Osgood came back into the kitchen, holding up a pair of Ossie's jeans.

"I found these *under* your bed," she said. "What a lazy boy you are. I knew I had emptied the laundry basket. Right, for that, you can wash them yourself. It's about time you learned how to."

She threw them at Ossie and they fell over his head as he sat reading at the breakfast bar. Lucy and his mother both burst out laughing. One leg was dangling over Ossie's face, with the end of it dipping into his bowl of Weetabix, slowly soaking up the milk.

Ossie got down from his stool, very bad-tempered.

"I hate all of you in this house. You'll regret it. When I'm famous, I'll disassociate all of you."

Ossie slammed the door as he went out. There was milk still dripping from his hair.

Ossie let himself into his grandad's, hoping there would not be much shopping to do this morning. He didn't want to be late, when he was going to the match. He couldn't decide whether the agony of watching Desmond play, when he knew *he* should be playing, was really worth being taken for a hamburger afterwards by Desmond's dad. According to Desmond, his dad was going to treat any of his friends who turned up to watch.

"You'd need to be treated," thought Ossie, "just to watch that cruddy player. No skill. Not like me."

"Crud" was the word of the week. It meant anything at all bad, or anything which Ossie did not approve of, which was the same thing.

Ossie jumped up as high as he could, which wasn't very far, and headed an imaginary ball into an imaginary goal.

" 'Goal! And Ossie Osgood has scored his hat trick with another unstoppable goal! That must be Goal of the Month, don't you think, Jimmy. Spurs are now beating Arsenal nine nil. Back to the studio.' . . . Oh sorry, Grandad."

Ossie had not seen his grandad coming out of the living room. They banged into each other, as Ossie was still milking the cheers of the imaginary crowd behind the imaginary goal.

"What's all this, then?" said Grandad.

"Oh, I was just pretending to score a goal . . ."

"I don't mean that, " said Grandad, taking something from behind his back. "I mean this!"

It was a typewritten envelope addressed to Ossie Osgood—at his grandfather's address.

"Oh," said Ossie, thinking quickly. "It'll probably be from the *Dandy*. I sent off to join their Desperate Dan Pie-Eating Club."

"What?"

"Mum says I haven't to waste my money on any more of these clubs, so I used your address so she shouldn't find out. But it's a really good club. You get this sticker . . ."

"I'll let you off this time," said Grandad, giving him the envelope.

Ossie took the envelope into his grandad's bedroom, putting the light on.

"I like reading things on my own," said Ossie.

"I don't mind. I don't want to watch you reading anyway," said Grandad. "Your lips move all the time."

Ossie could hear his grandad laughing at his own wit, but Ossie was more intent on tearing open the letter.

It was from Tottenham Hotspur Football Club. Ossie Osgood was being invited to a trial at the

Spurs training ground, Cheshunt. And it was that very morning.

"Grandad's probably had this letter for days and days," groaned Ossie. "I bet he's been trying to steam it open. Rotten cheat. I know his cruddy tricks.

"Oh, I wish I was eighteen, then I would be able to go."

Ossie stared at the dark, mysterious wardrobe. It was tightly closed today. He hoped Grandad had not locked it. He looked again at the letter.

Please bring boots with you.

Ossie jumped up, listened at the bedroom door, then turned the light off, opened the wardrobe and stepped in. He touched all the medals, uniforms and badges, then the cavalry boots, the shrapnel and the Iron Cross. He closed his eyes, wishing and wishing that he could be eighteen.

When he stepped out, it had miraculously happened again.

He was now in very smart casual clothes, rather than jeans, and wearing a leather jacket. In his hand was a large sports bag marked Spurs. Inside was a pair of boots. Size 9.

Just the size for a well-built eighteen-year-old, the star of his school team . . .

Oz ran home, worried at first that people might recognize him, but he was so smartly dressed as a man of the world, nobody did.

He let himself into his house, ran upstairs and got the most recent coupon from his pile of free train tickets. Then he ran all the way to the station.

"When you are eighteen, in perfect physical condition," thought Oz, "you can run anywhere. And it's good training."

Oz had been to White Hart Lane twice to see Spurs play, taken there by car by Desmond's father, but he had never been to the Spurs training ground at Cheshunt. He knew about it, having been a Spurs supporter all his life. He knew that it was about fifteen miles north of London in Hertfordshire, which meant he did not have to go into London itself. He was not sure if he could have made that journey all on his own.

"What am I saying? At eighteen, I can go anywhere!"

*

He managed to catch a London train, one which stopped at Cheshunt, just as it was leaving the station, and threw himself into the first compartment.

Flossie and her father were sitting opposite.

Oz tried to hide his head, bending down and pretending to tie his shoe-laces.

"Oh no," he thought, "I can't sit like this all the way to Cheshunt. I'll be too stiff to play football."

Very slowly, he straightened up. Flossie's father was reading something called *Stamp News*. Flossie was looking out of the window, admiring the countryside, so Oz thought at first, till he realized she was admiring her own reflection.

"Typical," said Oz.

"Sorry," said Flossie, peering over her spectacles, giving him her best film-star smile. "Did you say something?"

"Eh," stumbled Oz. "Topical. I said it's rather topical. Your dad reading about stamps, 'cos stamps are sort of topical, aren't they? I got one only today. On a letter from, I mean, just a letter . . ."

"How did you know I am her father?" said Flossie's father. Flossie sighed at this.

"When you collect on one topic," explained her father, "such as stamps with trains on, or stamps about birds, then you're called a 'Topical collector', so it's interesting you mentioned the word . . ."

"We're going to London for the day," said Flossie, breaking in, trying to change the subject.

"That's lucky," said Oz. "That's where this train's going."

Flossie burst out laughing. This was just her sort of humour.

"Where are you going, then?" she asked.

"Oh, just a spot of training," said Oz, modestly, patting his gleaming Spurs bag.

"Should I ask him?" said Flossie, turning to her father.

Her father looked rather mystified.

"You know, dum dum," said Flossie. "For my new collection?"

"Oh, yes, why not. Might as well get it started."

Flossie leaned across to Oz and gave him her very best smile. From her pocket she produced a little red book.

"Can I have your autograph?"

Oz was startled. He had not quite expected this,

but naturally he agreed. He didn't have a pen, but Flossie's father produced one, and Oz signed with a flourish.

The train stopped for only a moment or two at Cheshunt, as it is a very small station. Oz jumped out, beaming with pleasure.

"Imagine that," he said. "Signing autographs, and I haven't even played for Spurs yet. What will it be like when I score a hat trick . . ."

Oz stood outside the station wondering which way to go. He was suddenly feeling rather lost, and very young. On the train, he had felt quite confident and excited. Now he was alone, a long way from home, with no one to help him.

"Perhaps I should have brought my mum. She might be pretty stupid—well, sometimes. Well, that's what I say. But she is good at directions."

Oz thought about hitch-hiking, but he wasn't sure how you did it. Did you put your thumbs down or up? Or did you give a V sign? "If only Mum was here. She knows things like that."

He was beginning to think it was all a bit silly. Perhaps he should get the next train back home.

At that very moment an old bashed-up estate car stopped right beside him. It was one of those cars with wooden bits on the sides, but it was so old that plants and moss were growing out of the wood. An old woman leaned from the window. She, too, seemed to be covered in moss and bits of plants.

"You look lost," she boomed.

"Er," hesitated Oz. "Well, that's because I am lost. I never got my tenderfoot badge in the Boy Scouts. My mum usually comes with me when I go away from home, but this time I just, you know, I thought I'd try."

The old woman looked him up and down, as if fitting him for a new suit. He looked very tall and well built to her, but he was acting like a nervous eleven-year-old.

"Where are you heading for, chummy?"

"Eh, Spurs," said Oz. "Have you heard of them? Their training ground is supposed to be very near here."

"That's just where I'm going," she said. "Jump in."

"Eh, you're not having a trial, are you?" said Oz.

He knew that these days girls played football as well as boys, and had proper leagues, but if old women also played, that was going to make competition for places even worse.

"No, no," she said. "I just go to watch them training. I do like watching athletes at the top of their powers. Bimbo likes to watch them, too."

"Bimbo?" asked Oz.

Perhaps she had a son. More competition.

"My dog," she said.

There was a growl from behind him. Oz had not noticed that there was a dog in the back of the estate car. He was covered in bits of straw and moss as well. Perhaps they all lived in a barn.

"I have to keep him on a lead. The beastly groundsman throws you out otherwise."

She drove up a little lane and let Oz out near a large pavilion; then she parked beside several people who were standing about, watching the players practise.

"Jolly good luck," she shouted towards Oz. "We'll be watching."

There seemed to be dozens of pitches, as far as Oz could see, and also dozens of players, all in different groups, most of them being shouted at by red-faced men in track suits.

Oz went into the pavilion, clutching his letter. A man in a track suit took him into a dressing room and told him to strip off.

"You're a bit late," he said, "but you'll soon

catch up. We're all doing doggies first."

"No, no, I've come to play," said Oz. "You've made a mistake. I haven't got a dog . . . I'm a proper player . . ."

But the trainer had gone. Oz quickly took off his clothes and hung them neatly on a peg above his head.

On the bench, where the trainer had put him, was a sparkling white Spurs shirt, plus shorts and socks, all the real football clothes, neatly laid out, specially for Oz.

Oz could hardly believe it. He put them all on, then found a little mirror in the corner and took a quick glance at himself.

In the mirror, he caught sight of other players in an adjoining dressing room, also getting ready. One of them looked like Steve Perryman, the Spurs captain. He was injured that week, as Oz well knew.

"Perhaps he's come to see me?" thought Oz. "He might have heard about me. I might just be the player they want for the first team . . ."

Doggies turned out to be special exercises. About twenty very fit-looking youths, aged between sixteen and eighteen, were running up and down in rows, touching hands, then running back.

Oz was given a blue top, a piece of material like a shirt without arms, which he had to strap over his chest, and was told to join the youths doing the doggie exercises.

Oz was rather disappointed. He wanted the whole world, even if it was just that funny old woman and Bimbo, to see him play football in a real Spurs shirt.

He did notice what looked like a photographer on a far pitch, busy taking photographs of someone.

"Probably Steve Perryman," thought Oz. "Oh well, that photographer will soon be taking me, once they all see what I can do."

After the physical exercises the trainer, who was small and stocky with close cropped hair, sent one of the young players to the pavilion. He came back dragging a huge rope bag containing about twenty white footballs. Oz had never seen so many at one time.

"My mum's promised me one of them for Christmas," said Oz. "In real leather. My plastic one has got burst."

The trainer gave him an odd look.

"Did one of our scouts find you?" he asked.

"Oh, yes," said Oz. "But it wasn't hard. I was in the Cubs already. And I was Sixer."

"Come over here. Let's have you. You can show us what you're really like . . ."

The players had made a large circle round the trainer. As Oz walked into the middle, the trainer kicked one of the balls at him, very hard. Oz just managed to trap it in time.

The trainer explained that he wanted them to take a ball each, then kick it up in the air ten times without letting it ever touch the ground. Then they had to head it in the air ten times.

"Our friend here is going to demonstrate."

All the other young players watched to see what Oz would do. He had spent years in his back garden trying to keep a plastic football in the air, but doing it with a full-size football might prove a bit harder. It did seem very heavy.

Oz kicked it gently in the air with his right foot, but it fell on the ground before he could get his left foot to it.

"Sorry about that," he said. "These boots. They're new. Never worn size nines before. Usually I'm a four."

On his second attempt, Oz did it. He managed it twenty times in all, then he did twenty headers, without dropping the ball once.

"OK, clever beggar," said the trainer. "I want everyone to try now."

After that, he gave them other ball exercises to do: passing the ball in pairs, then in circles with one in the middle, then dribbling round a series of white posts, then taking free kicks and corners.

Oz found it all rather easy, but then he was a star player with his school team.

When it was his turn to take a free kick, he became rather too confident and decided to give Bimbo a wave, just as he was running up to kick the ball. He slid slightly on the ground as he approached it, and a few of the boys started to laugh.

The ball was going very wide at first, then in mid air it seemed to turn and swerve round a group of defenders who had been positioned near the goal-keeper as a wall. It went straight into the net, completely beating the goal-keeper. Several boys cheered.

"Did you mean that?" said the trainer.

"Course I did," said Oz. "It's the wave of the hands that does it. Gives your body central flugal force. Roy of the Rovers does it all the time . . ."

"Can you really bend the ball?" said a boy standing beside Oz.

"Easy peasy," said Oz. "All it takes is skill."

"Right, you lot," said the trainer, clapping his hands. "I can see we have some circus performers here today. But now we'll have a game. That'll separate the men from the boys."

This time, all the players took part. The apprentices, the youth players, those on trial, and the first team players who were doing special training, they were all split into four teams: blue, red, green and yellow.

"We'll now have two matches," said the trainer, "both on the same pitch at the same time. This is to sharpen up your reflexes and mental awareness. So you'll all have to concentrate. Is that clear?"

Most of the boys were utterly confused. Having

two balls on the same pitch, and two teams both playing in the same direction, is very complicated.

The trainer enjoyed going round shouting at every player who made a mistake, or lost his concentration, or followed the wrong ball.

Oz found it remarkably easy. Most of his playing career so far had been in the school playground, with girls all around, and with other groups playing at the same time. It had taught him a lot.

"Right, that's enough," said the trainer. "You're all bloody useless. Except you over there, that big flash kid, what's your name?"

"Oz, sir."

"No need to call me sir," he said. "But do it, all the same."

The other boys gave little forced smiles.

"Right, we'll just see if you are as good as Ossie Ardilles. You look bigger and stronger and a lot flashier. But we'll just see."

At last all the players were ready to play a proper game, on separate pitches, blues against the reds, greens against yellows.

Oz noticed that most of the little groups of

watchers had come to watch the game he was in. He was made central striker, his favourite position, but at first his team was defending, so he hardly got the ball.

He decided to go back when the other team had won a corner. Oz jumped for it in his own penalty area, nodded the ball down to his feet, did a one-two with one of his own midfield players, then sprinted up field, through the opposing team, did another one-two and screamed for a return pass.

He got the ball just on his own half-way line, so he was on side. He beat three players with pure speed, which left only two defenders to beat. They both came at him together, which they should not have done. Oz saw them coming and scooped the ball over their heads and, almost in the same movement, ran between them, hitting the ball on the volley. It screamed into the net, bending round the amazed goal-keeper.

Oz could hear the lady with the old estate car clapping gently in the distance. Then the trainer started shouting at everyone. He was blaming the two full backs for both going for the same player.

He stood screaming at them for a long time,

holding the match up as he demonstrated how a forward should be covered, how one defender should have forced Oz out on to the wing and away from danger, and how the other player should help. Oz was getting cold waiting.

"Oh, hurry up!" he said to himself. "Skill players don't have to bother with all that stuff."

The other team managed to get a goal back, a scramble in the penalty area when Oz had been injured, making it 1–1.

From the kick off, Oz noticed that their goal-keeper was off the line. While still in the centre circle, Oz shot so suddenly and so fiercely that it went fully thirty metres, right over the goalie's head. It all happened so quickly that the trainer said he never saw it, but he gave the goal just the same.

"I bet he did see it," thought Oz. "Just jealous."

The other team got a penalty. Unfair, thought Oz, the trainer just gave it to them, to make it a more even game. Oz was determined to show some of his real tricks this time.

He got the ball deep in his own area and did a little back flick, sending the ball over his own head and so beating two of their men.

He was going very near the touch line, right on the line, but just as the ball appeared to be rolling out of play, it hit Bimbo on the head, and stayed in play. Or had Oz meant it?

Oz ran down the wing, beating another three men by sheer speed. At the corner flag, he did some juggling with the ball, before putting it through the legs of their largest defender.

He then cut inside, keeping the ball very close to his feet, side-stepping several lunges, body-swerving his way to the edge of the penalty area. From a very acute angle, when it seemed impossible to even see the goals, he sent a rocket of a shot which roared into the top right-hand corner of the net.

The trainer whistled for the goal—and for the end of the match. The little crowd of onlookers gave a big cheer. Several players rushed up to pat Oz on the back.

Oz walked away modestly, determined not to be big-headed, not like some players he could mention.

Going over to the touch-line, he saw the old lady with the dog who had given him a lift.

"Jolly well done," she said.

"Thanks, Bimbo," said Oz.

Oz was sitting in the dressing room, putting on his clothes. He had had a shower with all the players.

Quite a few of the Spurs senior team came up and said, "Well played, well done."

"It was just luck," said Oz. "One of those days."

"Would you like me to recommend an agent?" said one of them.

"Oh, I don't think I want to be one of those. Spies, secret agents, never appealed to me. When I grow up, I fancy being a detective, if I can't be a footballer."

They all laughed, thinking it was some new, eighteen-year-old humour.

Oz picked up his dirty football clothes from the floor, as his mother had always told him to, though he usually forgot.

He saw that the rest of the players were putting the dirty clothes in a big wickerwork skip. It would immediately be taken away and all the clothes washed that morning, so he was told.

"I could do with that in our house," thought Oz.

Just as he was putting his clothes away, and

packing his boots in his bag to take home, two of the trainers came up to him.

"What you doing this afternoon, son?" said the oldest of them, a man with a broad Yorkshire accent.

"Might go to the school jumble," said Oz. "Or play in the street with my friends."

The trainers were looking at each other, rather puzzled.

"Or I might read my comics," said Oz. "*Champ* and *Eagle* come out today. It is Saturday, isn't it?"

"Forget all that rubbish," said the older trainer. "I mean, what might you be doing at three o'clock this afternoon? It looks as if we could have problems. We've got our three centre forwards injured and . . ."

"Oh no," said Oz, getting up. "My grandad's! I've forgotten to do his shopping! I meant to do it this morning. It's my Saturday job. I'll have to get home quickly before the shops shut."

Oz got up, grabbed his bag, and ran out of the pavilion and down the lane.

Behind him, he could hear the trainers shouting after him. It sounded something like "signing forms", or it might have been signing autographs, but he wasn't quite sure . . .

It was tea-time in the Osgood household. Ossie was making the tea for his sister and mother: beans on toast.

"Oh, is that all?" said Lucy.

"Well, it's more than you can make," said Ossie. "You need a recipe book just to boil some water."

"What's for afters then?" asked Lucy.

"Oh, Lucy," said her mother. "That is very greedy. Just wait and see what Ossie has done. I can smell something lovely in the oven."

It was rock cakes, though Ossie was keeping it a secret, just in case. He had learned to make them at school that week.

Ossie had got home just in time to mix up the flour, butter, egg, sugar and currants and then shove them in the oven. He realized when he put them on the tray that he had not washed his hands after travelling back on the train and then hurrying to do his grandad's shopping.

It had all been a terrible rush, but he had got it all done. He had even managed to ring Desmond and find out the school's score.

"I dunno," said Ossie. "I just rush round all the time, looking after people. If it's not Grandad, it's you lot. It's just go, go, go."

"Aren't we lucky, Lucy?" said Mother. "Having such a treasure."

"If only he did this more often," said Lucy. "He's just putting it on. I know him. He'll be horrible to you again soon."

Ossie was whistling to himself, standing in front of the oven with the oven gloves on. He took a quick look at the rock cakes. They were almost ready and had turned a rather dark brown colour, darker than they had been at school.

"How did the match go, Ossie?" asked Mother.

"Oh, triffic," said Ossie. "Really good. I was brilliant."

"I didn't know you played," said Mother.

"I heard they got beat nine nil," said Lucy.

"Oh, I mean," said Ossie, "I mean I did very well. Going all that way and supporting them. It wasn't fair really. The other team were so much bigger. You can't do much, after all, if you're small and weedy, like poor little Desmond."

"Well, I'm glad you enjoyed it, dear," said Mother.

"It was interesting, anyway," said Ossie. "A good experience."

"After tea, Ossie," said Mother, "I'm going to put on the washing machine again and do another load. So if you want your jeans done now, get them out."

"Oh, that's good," said Ossie. "Can you wash this shirt as well, please?"

Ossie went to his room and brought down a dirty Spurs shirt.

When he had got back to his grandad's, he found he had brought it home by mistake. Very strange.

"That looks rather big for you, doesn't it?" said his mother.

"Oh yeh, miles too big," said Ossie. "I got given it."

"What?"

"Someone I met at the match. A sort of present. It will do for when I'm eighteen. I'll just keep it as a sort of souvenir till, you know, till I'm eighteen . . ."